Write a card to your grandpa ...

- Inside the pocket you will find two writing cards and two envelopes.

- Open up the cards and write your address at the top. Then write to your grandpa, telling him how much you love him.

- When you have finished, sign your name at the bottom.

- Then put the card in the envelope. Write your grandpa's address on the front of the envelope.

- Put a stamp on the envelope and mail it. It will make your grandpa happy to hear how special he is.

Written by Jillian Harker
Illustrated by Daniel Howarth

This edition published by Parragon in 2008

Parragon
Queen Street House
4 Queen Street
Bath BA1 1HE, UK

ISBN 978-1-4075-5056-5
Printed in China

I Love You, Grandpa

Bath New York Singapore Hong Kong Cologne Delhi Melbourne

Little Bear and Grandpa were walking
by the river when Little Bear spotted a fish
darting through the water.

"Quick, Grandpa!" he yelled.

He rushed into the river, caught
the fish, and held it up proudly
for Grandpa to see.

Grandpa smiled. "You're fast, Little Bear," he said. "I can remember when I was as fast as you."

He started to cross the river and turned to Little Bear.

"My legs were once strong and speedy like yours," he added. "But now I've found an easier way to catch a meal."

"Really, Grandpa?" asked Little Bear. "What's that?"

"Well," replied Grandpa, "I'm more crafty now." He stopped on a rock.

"I stand here at the rapids," Grandpa said, standing very still. "I'm patient. I wait until the fish jump out of the water... straight into my mouth."

"Wow!" said Little Bear.
"I love you, Grandpa.
You're so clever!"

Just then, Eagle swooped down.
The beat of his wings ruffled the bears'
fur. They saw his sharp claws.

Little Bear ran straight up a tree. Grandpa smiled.

"I can remember when I could climb as well as you," he said. "My arms were strong. But now I don't need to run away."

"Really, Grandpa?" asked Little Bear. "What do you do instead?"

"Well," replied Grandpa, "I'm bolder now." When Eagle swooped again, Grandpa barked in his deep, gruff voice. He roared, and Eagle swerved away over the mountains.

ROOOOO aaarrr

"Wow!" said Little Bear.
"I love you, Grandpa. You're so brave!"

They walked on until they came across a slope, where the earth was softer and deeper.

"Watch me, Grandpa!" called Little Bear.
"I can dig myself a really good hollow to
sleep in through the winter."
And Little Bear began to scrape away the soil.

Grandpa smiled. "I can remember when I could dig as well as you," he sighed. "My claws were really sharp. But now I know a better way to find a hollow."

"Really, Grandpa?" frowned Little Bear. "But where do you spend the winter?"

"Well," replied Grandpa, "I'm wiser now.
All I need to do is to find a hollow tree."
He padded through the woods in front of
Little Bear. "Follow me," he called.
And he led Little Bear to a huge tree.

In the middle of its massive trunk was a snug hollow.

"I love you, Grandpa," laughed Little Bear. "You know so much."

Little Bear looked up at Grandpa.
"Will I ever be as crafty, brave, and
wise as you?" he asked.

"Of course you will!" replied Grandpa.
"Shall I start teaching you now?"
Little Bear nodded.

So Grandpa took Little Bear to the rapids
and taught him the crafty way to catch a fish…

...and the brave way to scare a bird away.
Little Bear learned quickly.

Soon soft flakes of snow began to fall.

"It's time to find us a hollow tree big enough for two," Grandpa said.

And he helped Little Bear to choose wisely.

Little Bear snuggled up to Grandpa.
He felt really good.
  "I love you, Grandpa," he laughed.
Grandpa ruffled Little Bear's messy head.
  "I love you too, Little Bear,"
Grandpa said.